Richard Carrick was a production employee in a chocolate factory from 1988 to 2020.

He has diplomas in copywriting and screenwriting from The Blackford Centre in London. He also has a diploma in advertising from The International Career Institute.

His favourite film is An American Werewolf in London. This film was the inspiration for *The Beaumont Werewolves and Vampires' Society*.

I would like to dedicate this book to my mother, Catherine Carrick, who was the greatest inspiration to me in life.

Richard Carrick

THE BEAUMONT WEREWOLVES AND VAMPIRES' SOCIETY

AUSTIN MACAULEY PUBLISHERS™

LONDON • CAMBRIDGE • NEW YORK • SHARJAH

A CIP catalogue record for this title is available from the British Library.

ISBN 9781528993432 (Paperback)
ISBN 9781528993449 (ePub e-book)

www.austinmacauley.com

First Published (2021)
Austin Macauley Publishers Ltd
25 Canada Square
Canary Wharf
London
E14 5LQ

I would like to thank my mother and father Catherine and Richard Carrick for what they did for me in the course of their lives.

I would also like to acknowledge my sister Paula, and my brother David as well as his wife Mary. My nieces Lorna, Fiona, Ruth and my great nephews Ryan and Jacob as well as my great niece Faye.

A special thank you to all the staff in the chocolate factory for the well wishes when they heard the book was going to be published.

I would also like to include my sister's friends and work colleagues for their support.

Finally, a big thank you to all the staff in Austin Macauley.

St Helens, England

Dad:

"Catherine, get up soon or you will miss your connecting trains to get you to Manchester Airport for your flight to Dublin."

Catherine:

"Right, Dad, I am up, and I will be out the door in twenty minutes. I am just listening to the song *Hungry Like the Wolf* by Duran Duran; the song is on the radio."

Location: O'Connell School, Dublin

Headmaster:

"Tonight, ladies and gentlemen, we have a teacher who is about to speak about the Irish school system, his name is Denis Martin. So, I would like you to put your hands together in making Mr Martin very welcome."

Audience:

The audience starts to clap loudly.

Denis Martin:

"Thank you, ladies and gentlemen, I would just like to thank everyone here for attending tonight.

The subject tonight is the Irish school system and what I have to say will upset a few people. The whole school system is fixed for you to fail. To be considered a genius in the Irish school system, a student will have to get the following results: an 'A' in higher mathematics, Irish and English.

Very few people can attain those results. About twenty percent of students get the top marks. The rest of the students will get the following results: seventy-five percent of students will get grade C and D in their final exams when they leave school."

"You cannot become a doctor, engineer, architect, or study to become a legal eagle with grade C or D. This means nobody could actually use their final exam results with the lower grades.

In football terms, it means getting knocked out of competitions at the quarter finals, nothing to show for all the hard work all the students would have put in.

We spend too much time on plays by William Shakespeare, Irish, and poetry. These subjects are worthless in the real world. There is not one employer who can use any of those subjects."

Audience:

At this point the audience start to applaud, however, a few hiss.

Headmaster:

"Thank you for your thoughts on the Irish school system. At this point people break up to go home."

Exit:
Mr Martin says goodbye to the headmaster. He decides to go to the main school, to use the toilet.

When he goes over to the building, he thanks God for the main door of the school being left open so he can use the toilet.

After he uses the toilet, he comes out the door, and walks along the corridor, to use another exit.

He then hears something, like a growl and looks back but sees nothing.

He then looks back again; he sees a wolf walking slowly behind him.

He starts to run up the stairs. The wolf starts to run after him. As he runs up the stairs, he falls. He picks himself up again. He starts running down the corridor. He is now panicking. He is breathing heavily. He is sweating. The wolf is catching up on him so he runs into a classroom.

He does not want to turn on the light, because it will bring attention to him. Suddenly, the wolf jumps through the window of the classroom door. The wolf stops in front of him. The wolf starts to snarl at him.

The wolf then jumps on him and starts tearing him to pieces. Nobody can hear him because everyone has gone home. The next day, his body is discovered by the headmaster. The headmaster calls the Gardaí, Ireland's answer to the police. The Inspector does not know what to make of it; he said it must have been a dog with rabies.

Dublin Airport

Two men are waiting for a British journalist to come from England.

One of the men is called Richard and the other man is called David.

While they are waiting, Richard says to David the following observation he has just made.

What should come over the intercom is "If you are bored stiff waiting for your flight, you should look at the female flight attendants' legs". All female flight attendants have got cracking pairs of legs on them. David agrees with Richard to do with his observation.

Finally, the person that they are waiting for arrives.

The woman shakes both their hands and says, "Hi I am Catherine and I am from St Helens, near Wigan in England.

"I came here to find out why so many people have gone missing or have been attacked by dogs with rabies."

David says, "Well I am just here to collect you and drop you off at the nearest hotel. Richard will fill you in on the details."

Hotel (INT)

A short time later, in the hotel lobby, after Catherine changes her clothes. Richard tells her about people disappearing in the Dublin and Co. Wicklow areas.

Richard:

"It started about three years ago. People just keep on disappearing. However, one night, I went out for a walk and I passed O' Connell School, where I saw a large wolf being guided into a van.

I followed the van and it went into Cathal Brugha Barracks. I took a photo of the man, and checked his profile on the Internet to see if he had anything to do with army personnel. His name is John Landis. I believe he has something to do with the missing people over Dublin and Co. Wicklow."

Catherine:

"Do you think the wolf had anything to do with the attack on Denis Martin?"

Richard:

"Absolutely, he did have something to do with the attack. I think he trained the wolf in some way.

I am going to Dr John Landis's meeting tomorrow night in All Hallows College. He takes charge of a self-help group to get people to deal with the challenges they face in life."

Dr John Landis:

"Good evening ladies and gentlemen, I would like to welcome you to All Hallows College for self-improvement in areas in your life.

Today we have a lot more in our lives for some strange reason, a high percentage of people are just not happy. We seem to be all stressed out. All of us, in a recent report, are getting less sleep.

More people are suffering from being down at times. It does not have any boundaries. It does not discriminate against anyone."

"It affects people who are celebrities and who are wealthy. Grief also hits ordinary people with ordinary jobs.

No one knows why so many people are so unhappy, because they have so many material possessions.

My first speaker is a person called Richard Baker."

Audience now claps for Richard Baker.

Richard Baker:

"Hi, my name is Richard Baker; I suffer from not being able to live with situations from the past. I keep on reliving certain moments from the past I wished I could have handled differently.

My anger started when I worked for an employer who bullied me for two years.

He told me I was thick, stupid, not intelligent and I would not be able for certain jobs in life.

He decided not to pay my taxes so I could not get my dole payments.

I met him twenty-one years later. He tried to head butt me because I got the Revenue Commissioners after him. I do not know how anybody could hold a grudge for so long."

"I hate his guts and I hope when he dies, I hope his death is painful. I should not have let him get away with it. I think now he was mentally deranged when I worked for him.

I suffer from a lot of anger because I did not live up to values other people had and what they thought I should be doing for them.

I should have listened to my mother more often. She gave me advice on certain topics that I wish now that I paid more attention to. .

Even though she is dead now, I say to her photo that I am very sorry for not listening to her. I now know she was right in what she was trying to tell me all those years ago.

I miss my mammy a lot. It is hell not having her around anymore. The pain is just unbearable. I wish I had my mum around just to listen to her advice. Living without my mammy, is like receiving a prison sentence without the chance of parole. Most days are just endless and dull without her. Each morning I wake up it is just another day without her." Plenty of men feel this way when their mothers die.

"Going into work eases the pain. However, it is the same day, over and over again. I am working in a job for the last thirty years and I am bored stiff with it. If I left and went to another job, there is a good chance I would be bored stiff with that one. I am just fed up of working. All a good worker gets is more work.

Well, ladies and gentlemen that is my story and my struggle with everyday life."

Dr John Landis:

"Thank you very much, for telling us so much about all the pain you went through and still are dealing with on a daily basis."

At the end of the class Dr John Landis goes to Richard Baker, and tells him that he has a nice lodge between Bray and Co Wicklow; he can go for a break for a week. There will be all sorts of people he would be able to talk to and get certain things out of his system.

Richard says yes, he will go for a break to the lodge.

At the end of the class, Richard and Catherine go to the doctor, and tell him that they found his class very interesting.

The doctor says, "Thank you very much, I decided to start these classes because of the high suicide rate, and so many people are living on their own now.

"The members can get a lot out of their system.

"I hope you can both come to next week's meeting?"

Catherine and Richard both replied yes.

Richard:

"I have a funny feeling about the class, that there is something wrong."

Catherine:

"I agree that there is something wrong; I have an uneasy feeling about the place."

They later part and agree to meet the next day.

Later on, a fog descends on Connolly Station, which is a train station, at around midnight, when most the trains have finished. A rail worker is making his rounds and says, "Who is there?" When he hears a growl, thinking it is a dog, he looks for it. He calls out, "Here doggy, doggy."

Do not let the fog scare you. As the fog clears, he sees a wolf, so he starts to run along the platform towards the end of the station. He breathes heavily, trying to outsmart the wolf.

He jumps onto one of the trains, going from carriage to carriage.

He does not know where the wolf is, suddenly the wolf comes from another direction, because it came in through a different door, and savages the railway man to pieces. The wolf slowly leaves the railway carriage and goes down towards Fairview Park, and disappears.

The next day, Catherine and Richard decide to listen to the radio; the news comes on that a railway worker has been torn to pieces by something, maybe a wolf.

According to the local police, their line of enquiry is that a dog with rabies killed the railway worker.

Catherine and Richard decide to investigate this more thoroughly and decide that there is something strange going on in All Hallows College to do with these attacks.

A few days later, they decide to go back to another self-improvement meeting hosted by Dr John Landis.

Dr John Landis:

"I want you to welcome Mr Joe Dante to tonight's meeting. He is going to give you some advice on how to deal with situations in life. Put your hands together for Mr Joe Dante."

Joe Dante:

Hi everyone, my name is Joe Dante, and I am here tonight hopefully, to help people to get through life, easier than before.

I struggle to get over the death of my wife. Her name was Jenny. I loved her very much. I wish that I listened to her more. My left is so empty without her now. When she was alive, if I drank a can of soft drink, I could say that was a lovely taste. Now, when I drink a can of soft drink, I do not get any taste whatsoever.

Being a typical wife, she did a lot of moaning; annoying about leaving the toilet seat up. I can't figure out why this drives a woman mad. However, it does for some reason. She told me that I was totally clueless about women. I told her I was in good company with all men. She used to look gorgeous in her nurse's uniform. If I were to offer you this piece of advice to anyone who still has their partners and parents alive, just to appreciate them.

When they are gone, they are gone. At times, it is just horrendous.

When I go to the cinema, I look at so many people and I have just realised how lonely I am. I do not know what I am supposed to be doing.

I am a 55-year-old widower, and I am more scared and nervous at this age. Isn't that funny in an unusual way?

I do not know how long I have got to live. Will I live for ten, twenty, or thirty years?

I never know what I am doing; I can't seem to get anything right. I am sure a lot of people can't get to seem to get a handle on life.

When I go to the cinema and I come out at the end of the film, the darkness nearly kills me.

The pain that goes through me nearly kills me. I feel like screaming. There may be only twenty-four hours in a day, at times it feels much longer.

When I see passengers on buses looking wet and miserable, it only makes me feel worse.

My message to you tonight, ladies and gentlemen, do not put your happiness on anything in the future. Happiness is just an illusion; it doesn't actually exist."

"Appreciate everything that you have in your life, because when it goes, it will never come back.

I feel like a werewolf because, I keep on changing for the worst at certain times of the month.

Well, thank you for listening; I hope you have peaceful years ahead of you."

Audience:

At this point, the audience gives Mr Joe Dante arousing handclap about being honest about the death of his wife, and the pain he goes through on a daily basis.

Dr John Landis:

"Thank you very much for that inspiring speech. I hope everyone took something out of it.

At the end of the meeting, Dr John Landis goes to Mr Joe Dante and tells him that he has a small hotel in Bray Co Wicklow where people can meet to speak about how to deal with difficult situations in life. They even go for walks in Co Wicklow.

"I think you will find those meetings to be very rewarding, listening to people with similar problems and how they deal with them on a daily basis.

Don't worry, we will not say 'think positive'. That expression is very annoying. I do not think thinking positive actually works."

Dr John Landis:

"I will send you the details of the next meeting. Just leave your details with the receptionist please."

Joe Dante:

"I will go to your next meeting."

Dr John Landis:

"Thank you, I think the next meeting will do wonders for you."

Richard and Catherine go to Dr John Landis and say, can we go to the next meeting? Of course you can, replies the doctor, leave your details at the door. I will get my secretary to get in touch.

Hotel

After the meeting, Richard and Catherine go back to the hotel. Catherine invites Richard up to her room to watch the television.

Catherine:

"Where is the remote control for the television?"

Richard:

"I found it on the floor."

Catherine:

"Switch on the box please, and keep the volume low. I do not want the guests next door being kept awake."

Richard:

"I will keep it low."

Catherine:

"What is on?"

Richard:

"I will find something. I am fed up watching all those logos of the stations on the screen; it impossible to watch a programme on the television with the name of the television station on the screen.

Catherine:

"I totally agree with you, it is impossible to watch a drama without looking at those logos."

Richard:

"American television is worse than ours. During a programme, a poster for the following hour will come up on the screen. I found this out by looking at programmes on the Internet."

Catherine:

"Remember Richard, tomorrow is the night for the meeting to do with meeting other people down at the lodge."

The next night Dr John Landis greets Catherine and Richard and all the other guests.

He says that when people notice he has a tight haircut and short beard, people say he looks like a professor from the local university.

Dr John Landis:

"I would like to like to give a short speech to do with wolves.

In the past, it has been known for serial killers to dress up as wolves so they could attack their victims.

Serial killers have eaten children and claimed it was because they turned into a werewolf.

If people from a few centuries ago, burnt werewolves at the stake. Who can say they did not exist?

Maybe people took on characteristics, which made them change from ordinary people into something else.

Well, as you know, this is a self-improvement meeting for men, and possibly a few women will want to say a few words during the evening.

I would like you to put your hands together for Mr John Carpenter, he is the one who has black hair, and looks as if he has come to fix your plumbing."

Audience:

All the members of the audience clap for him to give his speech to do with what he has learned from his life experience.

John Carpenter:

"Hello, my name is John Carpenter, and what I learned so far is: I think the vast majority of people look after themselves and do not care about anyone else.

If any of you have children, ask them to do as well as they can at school, because it is the people who do well in exams that get treated better than students who do badly.

When I was on and off the dole, I found out who my true friends were, and I also saw people's true colours.

I was really alone when I was on the dole. Very few people cared. This is why students should try to get the best in exams, because you are on your own in the real world.

Most of the time, very few people will take care of you. You better know your stuff in all situations in life.

One day, your mother and father will die. You will be left to fend for yourselves. Your husband or wife will die, and you too will be on your own. All of us will have to face it someday.

Some people will have to face it a lot earlier than some other people. When people go home on their own, they could be living on their own for forty years.

If you are in a job and get laid off, will you be able to go to another job?

This is what everyone should be thinking about.

Now, if there is one thing I would never do again, it would be that I would never have asked a girl out on a date.

Asking a girl out is an awful experience, and then I had to put up with all the games girls like to play. The vast majority of women made my life miserable.

I really have no time for the feminist movement. The only time a female does something for a man, is when he pays for it in some way. I think today's women are impossible to make happy.

I think a lot of women are unhappy because of the games girls like to play. If women keep on playing hard to get, men will just get fed up with them. This means women who want to have someone in their lives will end up on their own.

Some men and women will end up spending twelve to sixteen hours each day being on their own.

After so many years of this some people will wish God will just go and take them.

Movies have played a big part in how people look on situations in life. I think movies have had a bigger impact than most people think.

In 1983, there was a film called *Shirley Valentine* and the main character says to her husband that she will not be making the tea at six o'clock again. The husband is shocked and say's the following: "I always get my tea at six." Shirley Valentine say's, not anymore. She is going to Greece for the sex.

I think this film was one of the reasons women stopped making a man's tea.

In 1989, a film called *When Harry Met Sally* with Meg Ryan who discovered a woman just wanted to moan all the time.

Richard Gere discovered in 1990, that Julia Roberts in *Pretty Woman* would only do something for a man if he paid for it in some way. This is like real life; the only time a woman does something for a man he has paid for it through some form.

In 1991, there was a film called *Only the Lonely* with Ally Sheedy and the late John Candy. John Candy's brother in the film tells him that a future wife will not do his laundry for him. The wife will not do what his mother does for him.

The brother only said what plenty of men have said about today's women. The only time a woman does something for a man is if he begs and pays for it in some way.

Later on, we had Jennifer Anniston giving out to Vince Vaughan for not wanting to wash the dishes, because he really wanted to watch the sports. I am sure plenty of men watching this would have said it is much easier to stay single and watch the sports, than to have someone nagging about the dishes. We can all do the dishes when it suits us.

Eva Longoria in *Desperate Housewives* would not stop nagging her husband to do odd jobs around the house. She even tried to get the plumber next door to do a heavy job for her. When there is a wife around, a man will never be unemployed.

When men saw these movies and television dramas, all they thought was getting involved with someone is too much hassle.

Between there is no tea, no laundry, having to do odd jobs around the house, women turning off programmes on the television, constant moaning about everything. Marriage or living with someone is too much hassle.

All of us men will live without the hugs and kisses and we can watch the sports and other programmes.

This means that economically, countries around the world will suffer because men and women will not help each other out.

Think of it, the grass has to be cut and the house or apartment will get dirty. Things around the living area will get broken. If they have to be repaired, this will mean having to spend money. If a man or woman has to pay, it will mean less money in their pockets. This will mean that they could go into some form of poverty.

I will give you an example, an employer asks a man to work overtime. He cannot do it because he has to do the ironing or the housework. He may even have to mind children because millions of women will not do the ironing and will demand for a man to do his share of the housework. This means a man cannot do his share of the overtime. This means less production leaving firms because all the men are doing housework.

I will give you one example; a machine produces 50 boxes an hour.

Fifty boxes and hour over ten hours is 500 boxes, multiply this over four days this is 2,000 boxes.

If they have overtime for one ten-hour shift and the men cannot do it each week, covering fifty weeks.

This means the firm has lost out on an extra 25,000 boxes each year in overtime, because a certain amount of men cannot turn up for work, because a high percentage of women have stopped doing all the household chores.

With women refusing to do the ironing and all of the housework, a high percentage of men have stopped doing the DIY.

In a recent report, at least one third of all men around the world are useless at decorating, painting, hammering nails into walls. The result we are paying for this is that in the UK, twenty-five percent of decorating and do it yourself shops will eventually close down.

This means that shopping centres will lose out on the rent from all these shops. Factories will close down and people will lose their jobs. Delivery men and women will also be out of a job because they will have fewer places to deliver to each day. The government will also lose out on sales tax. If the paint and wallpaper isn't being purchased and changed every couple of years, this means no sales which results in no tax.

So, when the feminist movement stopped doing the household chores, this meant that other areas would suffer because of them not doing the ironing and demanding men to do their share of the housework. To finish off, I believe anyone who puts their happiness on any goal is mad. A lot of goals which people have gotten have not turned to be great. I think just put your faith in God and take what God sends you."

Dr John Landis:

"Thank you for your very informative speech on living on a daily basis.

Over the next few nights, we will have more stories from different people."

Later That Night

After the meeting, Catherine and Richard decide to go for a walk to the nearest town, called Bray. The amusements will be closing down shortly.

As they are walking along the beach, with lots of rocks and stones, and listening to the waves of the Irish Sea, they decide to walk on the path. They soon hear a growl, and they look, however, they cannot hear anything.

Catherine:

"Richard, I think we should walk a lot more quickly."

Richard:

"I think we should run towards the amusements for cover."

They run very quickly in and out of all the motor vehicles. They can hear something running and growling behind them.

They run past the big wheel; however, they are cornered in the area where the bumper cars are.

The wolf has them cornered; they run for it and slide across the floor. The wolf runs after them and corners them on the waltzer. The waltzer starts up and all of the machines start going around. The wolf jumps onto one of the machines and gets stuck. The waltzer goes around and around in different directions.

The wolf is totally confused; Richard and Catherine run for their lives. When they look back, the wolf goes flying off the machine, into a building.

They hear some type of a whine or growl and the wolf goes off in another direction.

Richard and Catherine run to the place they are staying and start screaming and telling people what has happened. Staff and guests come running to greet them.

"What happened to you," shouts Dr John Landis.

"A wolf the size of a man tried to kill us."

Dr John Landis:

"I knew it! I have been trying to tell people that this wolf exists."

"Where is the wolf?"

Catherine:

"The wolf cleared off somewhere into the town, probably up the mountain, where it could seek shelter."

Richard:

"I have a feeling it will be back tonight. There is a full moon tonight. Now, we all know these animals are shapeshifters, and probably do not need a full moon to change into a werewolf. However, tonight, a person will change into a werewolf. He or she will have no choice."

In the bedroom later on, Catherine says to Richard, we have to look out for one another. Later on at eight o'clock, the clouds clear the full moon, and Catherine and Richard hear a cry of a wolf.

Catherine:

"What will we do?
I am scared not knowing where it is."

Richard:

"Let's stay where we are."

Catherine sticks her head out the door just to see if they are okay.

She sees a wolf running down the hotel corridor, she ducks into the room, and says to Richard, "Run quickly, the wolf is coming."

Then there is a loud thud on the door.

Richard:

"Let's get out of the window and go into another bedroom."

They get out to window, and as they are going along the ledge, the werewolf comes out another window and tries to attack them with his paw.

The two of them manage to get into another room and warn the occupants that the wolf is after them.

Richard and Catherine run along the corridor, with the wolf behind them. The rest of the occupants decide it is safer to stay indoors.

The wolf is chasing them around the hotel, up and down the stairs. They eventually they run into the lift.

They come out of the lift, and run towards the main hall of the hotel. They are near the kitchen; the wolf sees them and starts chasing the two of them around the room. Chairs go flying all over the place.

They run into the kitchen and get knives out of the drawers to fend themselves against the wolf.

They try running to the local train station, the wolf has them cornered. However, a man on his motorbike comes and knocks the wolf sideways with his back wheel.

The wolf howls in agony and runs off. Richard and Catherine jump onto the almost empty train because it is coming out of service. They say to one another that at least we are safe here. The wolf hits his paw of the window to let him know that he is still around. They know he is on the roof.

At the next station, the doors open up and the wolf gets in. The door closes before they have a chance to get out of the carriage.

The two of them run towards the adjoining door which connects the carriages together.

They are near the start of the train; the wolf sees that the train driver is on his own. The wolf decided to run towards the engine. The wolf savages the driver, and now the train is out of control. It is passing all the stations at an alarming speed.

The last station is Howth, if the train hits the wall, it will go out onto the main road.

Richard and Catherine decide to go to the back of the train for less impact; they know the train is going to crash into the main wall at Howth station.

The train crashes into the wall and goes off the track.

Part of the train crashes into the main station, the rest of the train goes crashing onto the main road.

Catherine and Richard survive the crash and manage to exit the train. An ambulance takes them to Beaumont Hospital. When they are in bed, side by side; Catherine says to Richard, "We are going to have to investigate this further."

We know that there is something suspicious about Dr John Landis. Tonight, we will go for a walk towards his office. I will check to see where his office is located."

Richard:

"I will go with you to see what the two of us can find out."

Later on, around midnight, they manage to find that the doctor's office is located on the other side of the hospital, close to a closed off ward.

Catherine and Richard look into see a place where the 'post-mortems' used to take place.

They look through a crack in the door and they witness Dr John Landis administering an injection into a person. The person on the table turns into a werewolf, and the doctor has him chained to a wall. Catherine and Richard are shocked and scream at him.

The two of them run off and tell the nursing staff that they saw the doctor administering a drug which turned the patient into a wolf.

The nursing staff laughs at the two of them. However, they have to investigate their claims that a doctor may be giving a patient an injection that is not needed.

They go down to the room and they see a costume of a werewolf. The doctor laughs at the suggestion and says he is getting prepared for a costume party.

Catherine and Richard decide to follow the doctor back to his home. With binoculars, they spy on him throughout the night.

During the course of the night, they install cameras in a house to gather information on him.

They wait in a van outside and slowly see him starting to go mad.

Dr John Landis howls out in pain. He starts ripping off his clothes. He tears off his shirt and then his trousers and underwear together.

He is totally naked and he starts screaming in agony.

The doctor starts to go down on all fours starting with his arms followed by his legs.

The back of his shoulders start to get much bigger. The middle of his back starts to burst out with his spinal cord starting to get larger.

Hair starts to cover his back. His legs and arms start to enlarge; he starts to scream out in agony.

"Why God did you do this to me? I am living a life of absolute agony. The pain is unbearable. Put me out of my misery."

His head starts to enlarge, his ears start to change into ears of a wolf. His eyes start to change colour.

His face turns into a wolf with his nose coming away from his face. He is now a fully formed werewolf. He leaves his living room and goes out the back door.

He sees Catherine and Richard in their motor vehicle.

Richard says to Catherine, "Let's move." The car moves very quickly backwards, and then forwards.

The wolf starts running very quickly after the car.

The car starts swerving all over the place. The wolf starts attacking the side of the car. The wolf jumps onto the roof of the car. The car comes to a sudden stop and the werewolf flies off the roof onto the path.

The werewolf runs off in another direction.

Catherine and Richard drive away, looking for safety.

Catherine and Richard go to the local law enforcement officers and show them their recording of the doctor turning into a werewolf.

The police tell them they have to get in touch with the local army base, because he is an army doctor.

The army and the police find the naked doctor near the zoo. One of the officers calls out to the doctor and has the following to say, "Who has been a naughty boy? We have been looking for you for some time."

The lads knew you were up to no good. However, none of us could prove it. The soldiers and the police decide to bring him back to the army barracks to interrogate him.

Officer Robert Bottin:

"When did you turn into a werewolf?"

Dr John Landis:

"I was attacked in Wales, by a wolf. Nobody would believe me, that a wolf attacked me.

I knew that there was something wrong. I woke up naked.

So, I decided to hook up cameras in my home in Wales to see what was happening. I saw myself turning into a werewolf. I decided to experiment on myself, trying to stop the transformation.

However, nothing worked. So, I decided that I was not going to live alone like this.

I decided to see if I extracted a dog's and a wolf's DNA and blood cells together and inject it into people to see if it would work. After a few attacks, it started to work. My injections started to work.

People started to turn into werewolves. You will find a few more of us out there."

Rob Bottin:

"Can you name the other werewolves?

Yes, I can, the other werewolves are Joe Dante and Richard Baker.

I asked them to go to Co Wicklow and attend my meetings to let them mix in with other werewolves.

They were attacked and they too survived, to have the curse with them."

"Why do you want to turn people into werewolves?"

"Think of the military using werewolves. They could drop ordinary people near military sites. Those people would turn into werewolves and tear apart other soldiers.

The great thing would be nobody would know which people would turn into werewolves."

Officer Rob Bottin:

"Right, we are going to have to arrange a trap for the werewolves.

We will bring the doctor to a house in Co. Wicklow. We will stay there until the other wolves come along."

The soldiers decide to set a trap for the werewolves. However, Catherine and Richard cannot go because it is a military operation.

The house is on a small farm in the middle of Co Wicklow.

A few miles away in a barn, Richard Baker and Joe Dante, start to scream in pain.

The two of them howl in agony, as the pain goes through their bodies. Their bodies start to grow into beastly creatures.

They eventually transform into werewolves.

They go in search of Dr John Landis.

The officer, with other soldiers, is inside the small farm house. They can hear howls outside.

Dr John Landis:

"You will never defeat them. They will be too strong for you. There are more of us out there. We will eventually take over the country."

The officer and five other soldiers are inside the farm house. They see the werewolves outside and they start to shoot at them. The shots create a lot of noise and the wolves go searching for cover.

When it gets safe for the wolves to come out, they start banging on the door of the farmhouse.

The growls of the wolves scare the soldiers, and they start firing. The werewolves decide to come in through the windows and start trying to strike the soldiers.

More shots start to fire out. The werewolf known as Joe Dante hits officer Bottin and kills him with one blow.

At this point, Dr John Landis starts turning into a werewolf. He says "Get out" to the other soldiers. The other soldiers decide to make their escape.

By a strange coincidence, they are met in a jeep by Catherine and Richard. "We decided to keep an eye out for you in case something happened to you. It's just as well we were looking out for you."

"This plan you had went out the window," says Richard. "We knew it would not be a good idea to be inside a farmhouse waiting for werewolves. Where could you run to, in an event of it going horribly wrong?"

Soldiers:

"We are glad you thought that way. We would be werewolf food tonight, if it wasn't for you."

"How many werewolves are following us?"

Soldiers:

"There is Dr John Landis, Richard Baker, and Joe Dante."

At this point, they hear a loud bang on top of their motor vehicle. They start shooting at the werewolves; parts of their bodies come through the windows and roof trying to attack them in their motor vehicle.

The motor vehicle manages to swerve, which sends the werewolves flying off in another direction.

When they arrive at the destination, far away from the werewolves, Catherine says to Richard, "We are going to have to kill them ourselves."

Richard:

"You are right; we will have to kill them, either in the Beaumont Hospital or All Hallows College."

Catherine:

"We will have to go back to another meeting, and start planning on how to kill the werewolves."

Next Meeting
Dr John Landis:

"Welcome to our meeting to do with overcoming obstacles in life, and what to do about it.
I would like to welcome Anna."

Audience:

Everyone claps loudly in the room.

Anna:

"Hi my name is Anna, and I am here to get certain things off my chest.

I hope my speech helps other people in the room.

I feel as if the world is against me. I can't seem to get anything right.

I was sitting in the cinema the other night, wondering what on earth life is all about.

I am not married and I do not have any children. All I do is, get up every day to go to work and basically make someone else rich. I have often wondered what life is all about.

I wonder why some people seem to get everything in life. The horrible people of this world seem to get things in life, while other people seem to struggle.

I do not know what to do with my life. I am too old for nightclubs and too young for senior citizens club.

What I have learned about life is that the majority of people only look after themselves. Any person who puts their happiness on anything is setting themselves up to have a miserable life. I think people from all walks of life do not know what to do to try and get life close to perfect.

We keep on changing all the time. Some people say that we are all like werewolves. We keep on changing so much that some people don't even recognise us. I hope my view of life has made a difference in your life. Now, I will hand the meeting back to the person in charge."

Richard:

"There is something very strange about that girl. She seems to be far too nice; I am wondering, is she a werewolf?"

Catherine:

"I found something strange in the way she looked at me."

Richard:

"Me, too."

Catherine:

"I am going to follow her just to see if there is anything strange about her."

All Hallows College

Later on, Catherine follows Anna, a gorgeous looking red head. Anna looks behind her but she can't see anyone. Anna walks along the corridors of All Hallows College.

There is a very cold feeling around her. Catherine is just behind her; however she does her best not to be noticed.

Anna walks along the walls of the college, with her finger going slowly along the walls.

She knows Catherine is behind her. Anna walks into one of the classrooms. She then hides in the classroom.

Catherine walks into the dark classroom. She looks around the room, breathing heavily, and looks nervously, hoping to see Anna without getting caught.

She then feels spit falling down on her head. She looks up and Anna is on the ceiling looking down on her.

She screams at Anna. Catherine realises that she is a vampire.

Anna:

"Come to me, Catherine, I will not hurt you. If I bite you hard, you will then live like you never lived before. The press has built up an anti-vampire agenda against us. You could say that it casts a bad reflection on us. Think of it, if you become one of us, you will have a great night life."

Catherine:

"Not bloody likely. I like my life the way it is. I heard of partying every night. I prefer to do it my way.

All the things you said at the meeting. I knew that there was something strange about you.

I never imagined that you were a vampire."

Anna:

"I said all those things to get my future victims. A lot of women would agree with what I said.

I would meet those women later in the evening, and I have potential victims who would live for eternity.

I came from Transylvania, years ago. I am so old now; I have forgotten how old I am. I can remain young because of my victims."

I met Dr John Landis, who is not as young as you think. He wanted his victims to be turned into werewolves. I wanted my victims to be vampires, so the two of us thought up the idea of a self-help meeting club for us to catch our victims. We decided to mix DNA and the two of us decided to take blood from our victims. Then we just played around with the mixture of DNA as well as the blood samples and the doctor and I could turn victims into werewolves and vampires.

We also take our victims from the Beaumont Hospital. This is where we started to practice in hunting our victims."

Catherine:

"That idea was very intelligent for the two of you to have."

At this moment, Anna goes across the ceiling on her hands and legs. She looks down at Catherine with her hair going down her face. In her accent, she utters the following words: "I want to kill you so I can prolong my life."

Catherine:

"I like my life just the way it is."

Anna:

"Sometimes it is the chase that excites me."

Catherine:

"You can chase someone else."

Anna:

"Very well, if you escape, I will not come after you."

"However, you will have to escape from a few of us."

Catherine:

"Let the games begin, you are not going to get me that easily."

Catherine goes running towards the door, opens it and goes running down the hallway.

Anna just looks at Catherine running away.

As Catherine goes into the yard of the college, three more vampires call out to her.

Vampires:

"Hello Catherine, our names are Faye, Lisa and Claire. We want to have a good time with you."

Catherine:

"The only good time you will get is by looking at your watch."

The vampires are dressed in long, flowing white gowns.

Faye is a beautiful with long blonde hair which reaches past her shoulders.

Claire is blonde with short blonde hair.

Lisa has short black hair. The three of them and Anna, show her their teeth and start to hiss at Catherine.

Anna:

"I want her and I want to taste her blood."

The three of them start flying around Catherine.

At this point, Richard passes into the yard and gets Catherine into the Landrover.

Richard:

"Catherine, it is time to move, let's get out of here."

As Catherine and Richard are driving through the gates of the college, the vampires and werewolves try to attack the car. Catherine and Richard manage to get back to the hotel.

Richard:

"After all that, we managed to get back safely."

Catherine:

"I did not think we were going to make it. This is worse than I thought I never knew that we have to put up with vampires, as well as werewolves."

Richard:

"We are going to have a struggle trying to get people to believe that we were battling with vampires and werewolves. We will keep it to ourselves."

Catherine:

"To protect ourselves, we will have to get silver. Not necessarily a silver bullet to kill the werewolves. Something silver we can fire into their hearts.

We will also have to get garlic to ward off the vampires, and a stake. Remember; do not invite them in to your room.

Vampires can only come in if they are invited."

Richard:

"I hope you are not out of touch."

Catherine:

"I hope not, I do not want to be out of time in trying to figure out how to stop the vampires and werewolves."

Richard:

"We will have to go back to the self-help meetings to try and spot potential new victims."

Catherine:

"Richard. That is a good idea."

Richard:

"I am going to enrol in a shooting competition with bows and arrows to get my aim in shooting a werewolf."

"I will attach silver to my bow and arrow and fire into the werewolf. The chances of getting a silver bullet for each of the werewolves and a gun are slim. So, the best option is for the bow and arrow."

Catherine:

"That is a fantastic idea, Richard. I will have to think of a few ideas so we can defeat the werewolves."

Richard:

"Let's go back to my house. It would not be safe for you to go back to the hotel."

The Next Day in Richard's House
Catherine:

"While we are waiting here to be attacked by either werewolves or vampires, let's talk about something to lighten the mood."

Catherine:

"Do you think there is true happiness? Do you think there is true love?"

Richard:

"I was thinking that the other day, while I was in the canteen at work.

I do not know if there is true happiness, because we keep on changing all the time.

People come into our lives and leave. Some come into our lives for maybe two years and others come for twenty years and leave.

Some people give us joy; others can make us go mad.

The problem is we keep on changing all the time.

We pretend that we are not changing all the time. However, we are changing and sometimes it is very difficult to deal with.

I do not believe we should be putting our happiness on anything, because circumstances can change and God could easily take people away from us.

I do not believe that people really know what they are doing. The novelty in everything goes after a while.

I do not know if there is really a true love for everyone.

To get married to a doctor or solicitor, you would more than likely have to be in their profession.

The price of true love would be you have to be a doctor or solicitor.

If a person is lucky, the only person who loves you for yourself is your mammy. You do not have to be on a certain income, or be in a specific job for to be loved. Your mammy will love you just for yourself.

So, I guess I do not believe in true love."

"I do not really believe in karma either. What goes around comes around to that person in a negative way in that person's lifetime. If you are nasty to a person, the nasty person gets it back later on in life.

I do not believe this is true for every situation. I know thugs or men, who were horrible people, seem to get on in life and get material possessions and luck which they should not have gotten at all in their lives.

I do not believe in karma; horrible people can do well in their lives and nice people can get terrible lives."

Catherine:

"That is very interesting; I think I agree with you.

I sometimes really wonder what is going on in people's lives. I think people really got it wrong in certain areas.

I do not believe people should be putting their happiness on anything."

Richard:

"Plenty of people will tell you that when they got into their fifties, they really did not know what they were doing."

Catherine:

"I hope we both get some inner peace as we live longer. I do not know if there is a cure for loneliness."

"I do not know if we really can be happy all the time.

I am beginning to wonder if we are really looking for our parents' love in another person or other people."

Richard:

"I agree with you. I think we are going to be all right tonight. I do not think we are going to be attacked by vampires or werewolves. For some reason, they are going to leave it to another night. The werewolves and the vampires probably want to hit us when we are least expecting it."

Catherine:

"Let's go to sleep, it is raining outside. The rain is bouncing off the windows."

Richard:

"Night, I will see you tomorrow."

The next night, Catherine, as a journalist, has to report on a feminist meeting by a feminist called Nadine, who wants women to stop doing anything for men.

At the meeting, Nadine walks onto the stage and has the following to say.

Nadine:

"Ladies, I am here to ask you not to do the following for any of the men in your lives.

- Do not do your men's ironing
- Do not do your men's cooking
- Do not do your men's washing
- Do not do the housework
- Make all the men do the home maintenance
- Switch off all their favourite programmes on the TV

When we do all this, we will eventually take over the family home. All our lives will be better.

Remember ladies you are not to let your husbands or boyfriends go to step aerobics with all those girls in their leotards. Looking at a girl in her leotard is a form of adultery. Don't let your husbands or boyfriends go downstairs on Sunday morning to watch Match of the Day either. Now it is time for me to leave see you next Wednesday for another meeting.

Audience:

There is a sort of a handclap from the audience. There are a few fellow feminists who cheer Nadine.

Richard:

"If there is one person who deserves to be either attacked by a werewolf, or a vampire, it is Nadine.

Richard meets Nadine and tells Nadine that she should be doing something for a man.

Nadine:

"Women worldwide should not do anything for men."

Later on, Richard and Catherine meet Nadine and Richard tells Nadine where he lives if she wants to come in for a coffee or tea, which will not be poisoned.

Later on, Nadine decides to walk home down the street. She can't stop feeling as if someone is following her home.

She calls out, "Is there anyone out there?"

There is no reply, she calls out again.

Nadine does not know that above her, there are three vampires called Faye, Claire, and Lisa, hovering over her. The three of them are ready to attack her. Faye comes down in front of her. Claire comes down beside her. Lisa drops down beside her.

The three vampires show Nadine their teeth and say, "We have a very good idea that the men of the world will not miss you."

The three vampires decide to attack her and bite her all over.

Nadine:

"Stop biting me you bitches, you are tearing me apart. The pain is killing me. What have I done to deserve this?"

They now know Nadine is a vampire and she will find her way to the other vampires in the city.

Nadine is now a vampire and goes out hunting for her next victim or victims.

The night she changes into a vampire, the pain she is in is pure agony. Her teeth come from the top and the bottom of her mouth.

Her eyes start to get bigger. Her hands start to change, with large finger nails coming out.

Nadine starts to hiss, and cries out in agony. This is the first time and it will certainly not be her last. However, she knows that she will get used to it in the end.

Faye, Claire and Lisa tell Nadine that they will have to kill Richard and Catherine. Those two know their secret and the secrets of the werewolves.

They want to kill Richard and Catherine. They know that they will have to be invited into their homes.

They decide to rent out a house near Richard's because they know he is letting Catherine share the house.

Richard and Catherine hear something at the window.

Kim, who is also in the house on an overnight visit, who happens to be Richard's sister, opens up the door to Faye, Lisa, Claire and Nadine. The four of them tell Kim, they have moved into the house a few doors away, and they just want to get to know their neighbours.

Kim tells them to come in to see Richard and Catherine, unbeknown her that they are vampires.

The worst thing you can do is to let vampires into the house, because they will be back to attack their victims, in this case, Richard and Catherine.

Kim calls upstairs to Richard and Catherine, and tells them to come down because they have company.

Richard and Catherine come downstairs and walk into the living room and they see the vampires.

Richard looks at them.

Faye:

"Hello, Richard and Catherine, just popped in to see how you both are. Later on we should have a bite to eat, to help us get acquainted."

Nadine:

"Richard, I would love to talk to you about equality and getting to know each other. I have my eye on you. The rest of the vampires say that they too would love to get to know Richard and to see if he has any secrets."

Catherine and Kim say that it is time to go to bed. The vampires say, "Do not let it be long before we see each other again."

Richard and Catherine say, "I am sure it won't be too long."

Kim leaves the next night and leaves safely to get her flight to France.

The next night, Catherine is in her room and she looks out and sees fog outside her bedroom window.

She sees Faye outside, waving to her to open up the window. Catherine goes into a trance and opens up the window. Faye comes into her room and so does the fog. Faye and Catherine lift themselves up into the air, a few feet into the air, due to hypnotic powers.

The two of them go spinning around in the air. The room is filling up with fog.

Richard bursts into the air and hits Catherine, and wakes her up from the trance.

Richard and Catherine go running out the door and down the stairs. They go out of the front door.

However, coming down the road in silky dresses are Nadine, Claire, and Lisa. The three of them show Richard and Catherine their fangs.

They hiss like mad. The vampires are dressed in long flowing dresses which look like night dresses.

The three vampires want a piece of the action. They do not want Faye to have Richard and Catherine all to herself.

Claire and Lisa decide to circle Richard and Catherine; they go up into the air and back down again. Faye joins them and they circle the two of them.

Their silky dresses start to blow into each other; Richard and Catherine decide to run for it. They manage to run past the gate and jump on to a waiting bus.

The three vampires start to fly beside the bus, on top of it and near the driver's seat.

They start to howl at each other. Faye says, "I want Richard." Lisa and Claire both want Catherine.

There is only one problem; they have passengers on the bus to deal with.

The bus stops and the bus driver makes a run for it. Faye goes after the bus driver and starts biting him, she says, "I needed a drink tonight." Then she breaks his neck.

Faye and Claire start on the rest of the passengers by blocking the door for them to get off.

They say to one another, "We will leave Richard and Catherine for later on in the night."

They too start to bite the necks of the other passengers on the bus. Blood starts splattering all over the windows.

Richard and Catherine make it out the side door, while the rest of the passengers are being devoured by the vampires.

Faye, Lisa and Claire start to hover outside the bus. Faye lets Richard and Catherine run. We will find them later. The three of us have been fed for the night.

Claire says, "There are more of us up the road, they will not get very far." Lisa agrees with her and the three of them fly off into the night.

Richard and Catherine are running, as quickly as they can, when suddenly, five more female vampires decide to pay them a visit.

"Hello, Catherine and Richard, you thought you were going to get away by running a few steps. You were wrong in your thinking," says one of the new vampires.

"Before we have your blood for our supper, because it is Saturday, we will introduce ourselves to you."

Mollie:

"Hi, my name is Mollie; the vampire to my right is Vanessa. The vampire to my left is Una. The one above me is Rochelle, and the finally, the last one is Frankie."

Catherine:

"I am sorry but it isn't good to see you. Richard and I have had a dreadful night."

Vanessa:

"Well it isn't going to get any better. By the time we finish with the two of you, you'll be wishing Faye, Claire, and Lisa had gotten to the two of you."

At this stage the girls decide to show Catherine and Richard their lovely fangs. They start to make unusual noises.

The four vampires start to look at each other and show off their fangs.

Mollie:

"Let's get Richard first and bite him to see what he tastes like."

Vanessa:

"Love to see what he tastes like."

Una:

"I will get Catherine."

Catherine and Richard start to run like mad. They run into a building and jump off the top floor.

Just as they jump off a large building, a truck passes by them. They jump onto the back of the truck.

They finally make it back into the city centre. They decide to confront Dr John Landis about the vampires, as well as the werewolves. They know that the doctor is getting the werewolves and vampires from the hospital for their goal of taking over armies by placing people who can become werewolves and vampires.

INTERIOR:
BEAUMONT HOSPITAL:

John Landis:

"Hi, Richard and Catherine, it is nice to know that you met my vampires. With my experience, I can take over the armies by planting vampires and werewolves into their military.

However, first I have to get rid of the two of you. As you can see just out the window, the full moon is coming up. It will not be long before I turn into a werewolf. If I do not get you, my gorgeous vampires will.

They are waiting outside for you. Tonight, they and all the werewolves will start attacking all of the patients."

"The pain I will go through will be horrendous. All of us are werewolves. We all go through the pain of depression, bereavement, loneliness, and some of the terrible decisions we have made in life that we cannot change. Every day we wake up and think about what we have done and cannot change.

At this moment, Dr John Landis starts to scream out in pain as he starts to change into a werewolf.

The moon has just started to come out. The doctor starts to go down on all fours. He cries out, "What is happening to me"; the pain never eases. The muscles come out his back, then along his legs. His feet stretch one at a time. His nails grow very long.

Every part of his body gets bigger. Hair starts to grow all over his body. His ears start to get bigger. His head starts to expand, then his nose. His eyes start to get bigger and change colour with the pain. Then his teeth get much bigger and he then starts screaming like a wolf.

Richard and Catherine start running out the door, down the stairs, through the corridors. They start to see werewolves running around the hospital, attacking the patients. The patients are running everywhere, trying to get away from the werewolves. However, they start running into the female vampires. The female vampires start pulling them up and start biting them. The vampires start throwing them from side to side. There is absolute mayhem in the hospital.

Catherine and Richard manage to go outside the doors of the hospital, where they meet the Gardai and the Irish Army waiting outside. The police and the army open fire on the vampires. They manage to wound some of the werewolves. However, the werewolves manage to kill some of the soldiers and the police.

Una turns to the rest of the vampires and says, "We will leave and come back to fight another day." The other vampires say that is a good idea. The vampires fly off into the night, with a loud shriek.

Richard says to Catherine, "Let's go for cover to my house. Later on we can figure out what we can do."

Catherine:

"That is a good idea."

The next morning, Richard says to Catherine, "I want to go to my parents' grave. I get a lot of inner peace when I go there."

Catherine:

"I like that idea; I will go with you tomorrow, to try to figure out what to do."

The next day, Catherine and Richard arrive at the grave.

Richard:

Richard lays down flowers and says the following:

"This bunch of flowers is for you, Dad, for walking into work in all weathers to do shift and the night shift to support your family. I do appreciate what you did for your family. Eaten bread is not forgotten."

"Mammy, this bunch of flowers is for you for all the work you did for your family. You did all the do it yourself, decorating, painting, cooking, ironing, cutting the grass, hovering, shopping and polishing. All you did was work. Eaten bread isn't soon forgotten."

Catherine:

"That is a beautiful thing to say Richard."

Richard:

"I always say that when I lay flowers.

Those words give me a lot of inner peace.

When I am in the cinema, it can be very lonely. When I am in work, it can be just as lonely. I do not know if there is a place that can give me inner peace. When I am at the grave, being alone goes away.

It does not matter which season it is, I always get a sense of inner peace. I know it is hard to die, we had joy we had sun, and we had seasons in the sun as the song goes."

Catherine:

"Do you find it lonely, being on your own, Richard?"

Richard:

"I do find it hard and sometimes being with others does not help. I do not know too many people to talk too.

"When I heard that school days were the happiest days of your life, I now know what they were talking about.

The pain of not being surrounded by people can really hurt. People need people even if they are not talking every minute of the day."

"Richard, I think we should go to the graveyard, we may discover the vampires there."

Richard:

"That is a good idea; I also want to pay my respects to my parents. I always get inner peace when I go to my parents' grave."

The Graveyard
(Next Night)
Richard:

"Catherine, the grave of my parents is over there. I want to put some flowers down. Well Mammy and Daddy, the first bunch of flowers is for you, Dad, for walking into work in different firms and different shifts and working in all weathers to support your family. I know people say that eaten is bread is soon forgotten. In your case it isn't, I appreciate what you did for your family."

"Now, Mammy, this bunch of flowers is for you and what you did for your family. You never stopped working all day and night. You got up to change nappies; you took care of us when we were ill with fevers. You prepared all our meals before we went out to school or work and then our dinners, after the day came to an end.

You also did the hovering, cleaning, washing up, mowing the lawns back and front, D.I.Y., painting and shopping. Without all your hard work, the house would have fallen apart.

My biggest regret is not listening to you about fashion. I now know you did it for my own good. I am now deeply sorry for not listening to you about clothes and fashion. I can't get those years back now and I am now deeply sorry for not taking your advice."

"When you told me that death was awful, and when you died, that I would wish you were here nagging me about wearing trendy clothes, you were right.

"Every day is pure agony. I get up each day and it is like a prison sentence without any parole.

"Dad, if you happen to see Mammy in the spirit world, say this to her. 'Hey did you happen to see the most beautiful mammy in the world, and if you did, was she crying? Hey if you happened to see the most beautiful mammy that walked out on me. Tell her that I'm sorry. Tell her I need my mammy. Oh, won't you tell her that I love her.'

"I woke up this morning, realised what I'd done. I stood alone in the cold grey dawn. I knew I'd lost my morning sun. I lost my head and said some things. Now comes the heartaches the morning brings.

"I know I'm wrong and couldn't see. I let my world slip away from me. So, hey did you see the most beautiful mummy in the world? And if you did, was she crying?

"Hey if you happen to see the most beautiful mummy in the world that walked out on me, tell her I'm sorry for not taking her advice to do with clothes.

"When she walked out on me, in other words, she died."

"I lost my head and I said some things, and I am very sorry for not listening to her. I can't get those days back. I really do appreciate what she did and I wish that I could have those days back. Dad, tell Mammy that I love her every day, even though she isn't here."

Catherine:

"What you said to her was just beautiful and I am sure she is listening to you in the spirit world. I think we will have to go. It is starting to get dark and I do not know which creature

63

will be waiting for us. Will it be one of the werewolves or the vampires?"

"Let's get on our bikes it is starting to get dark. We will start to cycle and try to get home in time."

Richard:

"That sounds like a good idea, I do not fancy being around here much longer with the darkness setting in."

Catherine:

"Quickly, the vampires are overhead, they are circling around us. Let's cycle very quickly to your place of work; it is the nearest place for us to get some shelter."

Vanessa: (One of the vampires)

"Let's get Catherine, he has a soft spot for Catherine."

Molly:

"Love too. Let's circle around Catherine, and grab her off her bike."

Road

At this point, Richard and Catherine are cycling along the road. The vampires are going in between the cars and trucks, trying to get Catherine off her bike.

The cars start getting in the way of the vampires, trying to get Catherine off her bike. Cars and trucks start to swerve left and right, trying to avoid the vampires.

Eventually, Catherine and Richard manage to get to the workplace, where they run for cover. They run into the factory and lock the doors.

Catherine:

"Everybody lock the windows and the doors.

"The vampires are outside the canteen." At this point, the remaining staff in the canteen starts to panic and starts closing all entry points into the canteen. There is panic in the canteen because no one knows what to do.

Molly:

"Look girls, they are scared stiff of us; they do not know what to do."

Rochelle:

"That is to our advantage; we will try and outsmart them just before the sun comes up."

Una:

"That sounds like a good idea. I am very thirsty and I want my share of blood tonight."

Frankie:

"I am going to fly by the window to see how many people are inside the canteen. I just had a quick look and it is about twenty."

Vanessa:

"That is an easy number for us. Maybe, if we get one of those workers outside, the others will follow?"

Mollie:

"I know what we will do; I am going to walk along the window and look into one of the men's eyes and try to put him under my spell."

Rochelle:

"That sound like a brilliant idea."

Canteen:

Inside the canteen, the people are running all over the place, trying to stop the vampires from running all over the place. Two of the workers, Anne and Sylvia, start to push the chairs in front of the doors, so to block the entrance to the canteen. The windows start to break under the pressure. However, the vampires can't go into the canteen unless they are invited in.

Mollie:

"Let's go, we will come back another night, when they come out, we will get them."

At this point, the vampires fly off in the direction of All Hallows College, to meet the rest of werewolves and vampires.

Canteen:
Richard:

"Let's go when the sun comes out, they will be fast asleep by then.

Catherine agrees, and we will have to think of a plan to get rid of those werewolves and vampires."

Catherine:

"I want to go to Dublin Airport tomorrow night to see if we can get stakes and garlic. I ordered them a while back. I did not tell you what I ordered. If someone told me a few weeks ago, I would be battling werewolves and vampires in Dublin... The two of us will have to do something about it. I hope they don't follow us tomorrow night. I hope the vampires are tucked away in their little coffins."

Next Night in the Canteen
Sylvia:

"I am going out for a breath of fresh air, Anne. I doubt that they will come back. They have got better things to do than to sink their teeth into our necks."

Anne:

"I totally agree with you, they were probably only after Richard and Catherine. Mind you, having to battle the vampires last night, we better go to the union and ask them about our job descriptions. Battling vampires is not on the list."

Smoke Hut:
Sylvia:

"It is nice to get out of the factory for a while. I will never get over last night."

At this point Sylvia turns around and sees Mollie, staring into her eyes and says to her, "You were wrong, we were not just after Richard and Catherine. We want all the employees. All of us girls are very thirsty for some blood. I am going to start with you." At this point, Mollie bites into Sylvia's neck. Sylvia starts to scream, in agony.

The rest of the vampires arrive and they see Anne. They start chasing her through the yard of the factory. Una sees her and starts to chase her, in between the cars and trucks.

Una:

"She is mine, I am very thirsty. It has been ages since I have had a drink and I want my drops of blood now."

Vanessa:

"Go ahead Una, I will not stop you, make my day as well as yours and finish the female off."

At this point, Una jumps down on Anne's back and bites her from behind. Anne is in complete agony.

Una:

This is me, knowing me, knowing you.

There will be no more tears in my eyes for these people; all of us have a job to do. We all want the same thing. We will help Dr John Landis and all werewolves and vampires will attack and take over certain defence forces of the world. We will control everything.

Vampires:

At this point, all the vampires are up in the sky and decide to move on. Let's go back to Richard's house to see if they have come back.

Richard's House:

"All right Catherine, we will stay here tonight and try to figure out what to do. I really do not know what to do. I do not know where we are going to get garlic and a stake to finish them off. I think we may have to finish them off with holy water."

Catherine:

"That sounds like a good idea. We will go to the church and get a few bottles of holy water, and we will get the priest to bless the water."

Richard:

"As long as we are in the house, and we do not invite them in, we should be okay. The only way they can come in is if they hypnotise us."

Catherine:

"As long as we have to share a few hours together, let's have a chat of what we both thought was overrated and what were the biggest disappointments that we have gone through in life."

Richard:

"If I were to live life again, I would never have bothered with the dating scene. I thought it was very overrated and I did not know why people wanted to go out on dates.

The whole dating scene gave me more headaches and going out on dates, made me miserable. The second thing I have learned about life is that work is very overrated.

Most jobs are boring, they call jobs a career now; this just glosses it over. All we are doing is making someone else rich, including the government.

I think I would rather go back to school, at least I was learning something each day which made the day a bit more interesting. When I go to work, it is basically the same thing each day.

I think when people get into their fifties, they realise just how much we spend helping someone else achieve their goals, and people start to resent it."

Catherine:

"I did not realise how many people would come into my life and keep on leaving. If I had of known this, I would not have gotten too close to people. Deep down we do not know who our friends are. Certain people I have known through the years, tried to knock my confidence.

I think deep down, we should not know about certain things. If we did know, all of us might find life more unbearable. If I were to live life again, my advice to anyone would be: do not put your happiness on anything.

I feel a lot of goals people have achieved through their lives didn't give them the satisfaction they thought they were going to get. I think deep down, we are all on our own and not to be expecting people to help you out. Lots of people expect other human beings to start taking care of them.

As I entered my fifties, I think life starts to get harder. None of us know when we are going to pass to the other side. I think when we get into our fifties, we are really playing extra time in a football match and we could be substituted at any time."

Richard:

"I understand where you are coming from Catherine. I firmly believe that the only person who loves you for yourself is your mother. Everyone else, there is some sort of a price. To get married to a doctor, you have to be a doctor. Get married to a solicitor, you would more than likely have to be a legal eagle. There is always some sort of a price a man has to pay for marriage, if it is not income, it could be status or education."

Catherine:

"I think happiness is just an illusion, I do not believe it actually exists. I think people should be going for contentment. I also think love is just an illusion as well, we can fancy so many people.

This is why so many people get confused about life and happiness. The vast majority of people just look out for themselves and no one else comes into the equation.

I think this is one of the reasons why so many people are unhappy, especially when people realised how many people were out for themselves.

People think that what makes them happy will make them happy all the time. I think this is a mistake, we all have to take a break from things that make us happy or those things will not make us happy anymore."

Richard:

"Well at least that conversation has taken our minds of the vampires, which are more than likely close by. I would love to know where the werewolves are, tonight in Dublin. I bet they are staying inside some building tonight. You have got to see the weather outside. It is raining cats and dogs, and if we do not keep our eyes open, it will more than likely turn into raining vampires and werewolves.

Outside the House

A scratching starts to come down the window, there is a fog surrounding the garden. The rain is pounding off the window and the paths.

Mollie:

"Invite me in, Richard, or even better, come outside. If we come together, I can show you the meaning of heaven. Why would you want to go into the job that you think is boring you to death, taking all of your life for so many years? Yes, I did hear your conversation. In fact, all the girls heard your little chat with Catherine.

"Come to me, look into my eyes and we can have all the pleasure we both want." At this point, Richard is under Mollie's spell and he goes towards the window.

Catherine:

"No, Richard, stay away from her, she's got the look." Richard opens the window and tells Mollie to come in. Mollie comes into the room and at this point, Catherine knocks Richard out with a vase so he can come to his senses.

Inside the Room

Just as Richard is starting to wake up, the other vampires come into the room; Faye, Claire, Lisa, Una, Vanessa, Rochelle and Frankie. Not only do the vampires come into the room, so does a lot of fog. It starts to get very difficult to see one another.

Richard:

"Quickly let's get out."

Richard and Catherine run down the stairs and the two of them fumble with the keys of the door. They get out the main door and then the front door. They run down the road very quickly, panting and really scared. The vampires come out of the house, looking for them.

Mollie:

"Let them run, we can get them another night. I haven't had this much fun in years, scaring the daylights out of people. Anyway, there will be daylight sun in an hour and we can't be away from our coffins, or we will not see another day.

Richard and Catherine know we are a little dangerous. In fact, I think they both know that we are really dangerous."

All Hallows College
Dr John Landis:

"Good evening friends, werewolves and vampires. As you can see, we had a close call. Our secret was discovered and we will have to leave Dublin. We will have to go to Blackpool in England.

We have a choice of so many people because it is a tourist destination for so many people. We will be able to take over so many people by turning them into werewolves and vampires."

At this stage, Mollie, the blonde female vampire, starts to fly around the hall. She is quickly joined by Una, the red headed vampire, the one who has a temper which matches the colour of her hair. Vanessa starts to hiss at everyone with her black hair going into a long length as she starts to fly upside down.

Frankie and Rochelle decide to walk along the walls.

The rest of the vampires start to join in. All the rest start to turn into werewolves. The werewolves start to howl in pain.

Dr John Landis:

"Tomorrow, we are going to celebrate our last night in Dublin by going to a theatre called the Olympia. We will go out on a high. See you next Wednesday in the theatre."

Inside the hall, the werewolves and vampires do not know that Catherine and Richard are listening and watching everything that the vampires are doing.

Richard:

"Right, Catherine, we will have to set a trap for the werewolves and vampires tomorrow. I do not know what we are supposed to do. I can't get any silver bullets. The only thing I can do is get holy water for the vampires."

Olympia Theatre

During the performance, the werewolves and vampires started to get restless because they want to be satisfied.

One by one, all the girls start to turn into vampires.

The full moon starts to come out and the rest turn into werewolves. A lot of howling and pain starts to go through the vampires.

People start to scream and panic and start running all over the place. People start running for the exits. They start to trample over the rest of the people in the theatre. The werewolves start to attack the people who can't get out. The vampires start to suck on the necks of all the trampled people. The vampires and werewolves are having a field day.

The rest of the people start to exit the theatre.

Richard:

"Quickly, everyone pull down the shutters and close the doors."

The doors are shut very quickly. The werewolves are trying to get out with the vampires. There is panic on the streets; buses and cars swerving to stop hitting one another. People screaming at other people to get out of their way, cars start crashing into other vehicles. The werewolves and vampires finally crash out of the doors of the theatre. They start to jump onto cars and start to snap at people as they make their break for it. The vampires go back to the college and the werewolves join them later.

Dr John Landis:

"Well, werewolves and vampires, we have to leave Beaumont in Dublin. We will go to Blackpool in England over the next few days. Well, my female vampires, a number of coffins have been put on hold for you to be transported by ship to Wales. Then your coffins will be transferred to the train to Manchester, then onto Blackpool.

There is nothing more we can do in Dublin. We will have to find new victims in England. We will eventually take over the armies of the world by having so many werewolves and vampires in their ranks. They will not know which person is a vampire or werewolf. They will turn on one another.

Let's go to bed and get some rest. There will be a long journey in front of us and we need to get some rest tonight.

Army Headquarters
General Jack Dunne:

"I have invited Catherine and Richard tonight to our meeting. As you know, we have had Dr John Landis under supervision. We know he is responsible for turning ordinary people into werewolves and vampires to take over armies of the world.

Now we have planted listening devices to track down what the doctor is up to. We know from listening into his conversations. We have learned that he has implanted a tracking device into the vampires and werewolves to track them. They probably do not know that they are being tracked; however, we are not too sure. We do not want to get in touch with the British Army to tell them that there is a group of werewolves and vampires going over to Blackpool to take over their army. They would think we were mad. So I am going to ask Richard and Catherine to go to Blackpool and keep an eye on the Dr John Landis and to see what he is up to."

Blackpool Train Station
Richard:

"Well, Catherine, at least we have arrived in Blackpool. We will have to go to our hotel and check first to see where the good doctor is checking in. I will get a taxi and follow the doctor."

Richard:

"I checked up on the doctor and I overheard that he was staying in a hotel near the seafront. The army have gotten in touch and told us that he has taken over a funeral home."

Catherine:

"That would be a cover for his vampires, so he can check up on them; he can get away with having so many coffins and nobody will think twice."

"I wonder where he will go; he will probably go to where there are a lot of people in one area."

Richard:

"I think you could be right. I wonder when he will strike out and get his next victim or victims.

I am just looking at the weather and it is horrendous. The wind is very loud, and the waves are hitting the rocks at the front of the beach. It is horrendous, the weather, it would be foolish for anyone to go out tonight."

"They would not sell too many umbrellas here tonight or any night. The umbrellas would not stand a chance."

Catherine:

"Over the next few days, we are going to have to do our homework on Dr John Landis. The two of us will have to go to a private detective to get some sort of bugging devices to track him."

Richard:

"That's a good idea; I think we should get some rest. I am exhausted from the travelling today."

Catherine:

"That's sounds fantastic to me. I am bushed; I am dying for some shut eye."

Inside Richard's Room

There is a scratching on Richard's window. Richard hears, "Come here Richard, you know you want me." He hears whispering in his ear, "Come to me. Touch me where you want to touch me. You know you want me." Richard goes to the window and pulls back the curtain. He sees Vanessa outside the window, with fog surrounding her.

Vanessa:

"Come to me, Richard, we can have a bite to eat, so to speak. You will come into my life and you will not have to live this very boring life. We need more male vampires in our society. We are into equality. Do you know, sometimes it gets boring just hanging out with the girls?"

At this point, Vanessa starts to hiss and hiss and starts to drive Richard mad. Richard starts looking into Vanessa's eyes and says to her: "Come into my room."

Vanessa:

"Thank you Richard, I was hoping you would say that to me for a long time. Here I am, once again. Vanessa starts to walk towards Richard and he goes backwards into the bathroom. He goes back into the bath which is full of water and Vanessa starts to start to kiss him. At this point, Catherine bursts into the room, using her spare key, and drags the vampire off her. Vanessa goes flying into the wall. Catherine slaps Richard across the face, to knock him back him to his senses. "Quickly, let's go to my room." Richard goes to Catherine's room.

Vanessa:

"I will be back for you later on Richard; you know you can't resist me. It is only a matter of time before you are mine."

Catherine:

"You left your suitcase here in my room; get changed and get some dry clothes on you. Tonight we will stay in my room for safety. We will go to St Helens tomorrow to see if we can get a private detective. St Helens is about one and a half to two hours train ride from Blackpool."

Richard:

"That's what we will do, and hopefully she will be good. I am glad that I am here with you, Catherine. As I am looking out the window, there is total darkness except for a few lights. At times, I really hate the dark evenings. Sometimes it feels that there is no hope for people and certain situations in their lives. Everyone thinks if they were living a different life, their lives would be so much better. Sometimes, the darkness can knock the stuffing out of a person.

Tomorrow we will get an early start to see the private investigator."

Private Investigator's Office
Paula Anne:

"Hi, my name is Paula and I would like to welcome you, Richard and Catherine, into my office."

"What can I do for you, where can I help?"

Richard:

"What I am going to say is going to sound very strange. So I will get to the point straight away. Catherine and I are tracking a person called Dr John Landis, who has a secret drug to turn people into werewolves and vampires to eventually take over armies of the world. At the moment, he is in Blackpool and we want you to bug his room to find out where the next attack will take place."

Paula Anne:

"Now that is the strangest request I ever heard in my life."

Richard:

So you believe the story?

Paula Anne:

"I didn't say I believe the story, however, if you pay my fee, I will start to believe it if you believe it."

Richard:

"Great, when can you start the investigation?"

Paula Anne:

"I will start tomorrow, I will explain to you what I do and the gadgets I use to listen and track people. However, I want you to transfer my fee for the next few days to this account."

Richard:

"That sounds good to me; Catherine and I will be back tomorrow."

Odeon Cinema

Next night, outside the Odeon Cinema in Blackpool, a man is waiting for his date. The night is terrible, the wind is blowing really hard and the rain is pounding off the road and pavements. He is waiting for his date, who is late. He is starting to get annoyed because he knows she is doing this on purpose.

He is freezing and soaked to the skin and he knows he will be watching the film soaking wet.

The girl finally arrives and says the most worn-out phrase out of every woman's mouth. "Sorry I am late."

Man:

"You made me miss the coming attractions. I never miss the coming attractions. Not only that, I am freezing cold and soaked to the skin and you honestly think I am going to watch a film with you."

Woman:

"Right, I will go home."

Walking home, the woman starts to get worried because a strong wind starts to hit her and blows her all over the place. She starts to get worried and frightened. She hears a sound of a bin being pushed aside.

Woman:

"Is there anyone there? I am armed you know. You better leave."

Lisa:

"Yes, there is someone here beside you. We are the sexy, naughty, bitches. All of us vampires are very hungry and thirsty and we have not been fed in a while. You look very nice in your lovely outfit."

Claire:

"Not that your lovely outfit in going to be on you for that long."

Faye:

"You shouldn't have kept your date waiting; don't you know it is very annoying having to wait for people to turn up for visits to the cinema or anywhere for entertainment in the evening time?

Lisa:

"I bet you the other girls are sorry that they did not come out tonight for such a lovely feast. Some people may say, the late-night vampires get the worm."

Woman:

"Leave me alone or I will scream and people will hear me."

Claire:

"Go ahead; you can scream all you like; there isn't anyone around to save you."

Faye:

"Let's go girls, and have some fun tonight."

At this point, the vampires go down on the woman and sink their fangs into her neck and arms.

Lisa:

"Right, now girls let's see where Richard and Catherine are. I think they are up to something. I want to get my teeth into the both of them."

Paula Anne's Office

"Well, Catherine and Richard, so you want me to track down this doctor, who is going to turn into a werewolf at some stage, I guess you want me to spy on him.

Richard:

"Yes, that is what Catherine and I want you to do and how are you going to do it?"

Paula Anne:

"I am going to tell you what the job involves and what I can and can't do. Here is how I will prepare for the job. After

I keep an eye on this doctor, probably for days, I will probably die of boredom and I will be in agony, not being able to use the bathroom.

This is what I can't do: secretly record confidential communications on the telephone or in person. This can result in a fine or even a prison sentence.

This may result in a civil damages and I may be subject to a restraining order.

Now I can listen in on conversations in public places and some information may pop out. I will have a recording device on me that will pick up the conversations for me to listen to later on."

In my investigation, I will use a tele-recorder; this is a device for recording phone conversations. All I need to do is to plug a cable into any phone outlet where the conversation is taking place. Then regardless of the outlet I use, even if it is in the basement or garage, the recorder will automatically begin to record both sides of the conversation when someone picks up the phone anywhere in the house. The recorder switches off automatically at the end of the conversation.

Neither party in the conversation will know any recording is taking place.

I also use credit card size recording equipment. I can place bugging devices in mobile phones integrated with the skeleton of a professional recording system, with an invisible microphone under its loudspeaker. With further amplification, I will be able to record almost inaudible conversations rapidly and reliably.

I will also place bugging devices in watches, pens, buttonholes or tiepins, equipped with various types of additional amplifiers.

There is spaghetti microphone, and a cable eavesdropping system, I can hear conversations in an adjacent room loud and clear. I will need a special drill to complete the setup."

Catherine:

"Is that it?"

Paula:

"No there is more, this is a stethoscope and it is very sensitive and it can pick up the sound waves of a conversation through walls of up to 50cm.

You can purchase wireless transmission yourself but it would be better if you let the professionals do it. As some people say DIY does not stand for do it yourself, it actually stands for destroy it yourself.

I will also get information using wireless-eavesdropping, I will be using an ultra-long wave-transmitter, and I will set it up anywhere in the building.

Every wall socket is a potential eavesdropping station, and I can change the location at will. This system is suitable for short and long-term use and it is hardly detectable by detection devices because ultra-longwave transmission does not produce radio emissions.

Catherine:

"There seems to be a lot of work involved. I would like to go with you tomorrow to see more of what you do, and to pick up more information on the devices you use."

The Next Night
Paula:

"Well here we are, in my van, with a lot more equipment. We have external eavesdropping and monitoring systems abound. Many of them are highly sensitive and are difficult to detect, and cover a wide range of up to 1,200m.

Examples include the parabolic directional microphone, amplified by a parabolic mirror that focuses the sound waves on an electret microphone, making adjustments to the conversation source possible. Its range is about 100m and it filters and eliminates noise."

Catherine:

"What is this microphone for?"

Paula Anne:

"This directional microphone picks up the conversation from up to 70m away. It is small (240 multiplied by 20mm). It is ideal for video use, and it is also usable for different covert operations.

The covert directional microphone can be used in an umbrella. This umbrella is customised so that its tip has a highly sensitive directed microphone and can pick up conversations 50m away, distinctly and loudly.

Catherine:

"Anymore gadgets that you have in this van?"

Paula Anne:

"I have a laser eavesdropping system for recording conversations secretly from opposite buildings, 250m apart. It is discreet and has automatic focusing for beam stability and higher recording quality. I may put a laser transmitter and receiver in the same location."

Catherine:

"You can tell me later all the rest of the information on how we can track the doctor."

The next night, a tourist gets off the train in Blackpool train station. He is the last to get off the train with his small case.

The darkness makes it very hard for him to see anything. The fog has started to fall which means he can't see too far in front of him. He hears a growl.

Male Tourist:

He calls out, "Who's there?"

He then hears another growl. He calls out the following: "If you do not answer me, I will make a complaint to Blackpool Tourist Office. He then hears another growl."

Male Tourist:

"I will even go further; I will make an official complaint to the Prime Minister of England."

He then sees a wolf coming slowly towards him.

"Good God, what is that?
It's a hound from Hell."

He then drops his small suitcase and goes running towards the doors, he goes inside and starts to close the doors and shutters very quickly. He starts to scream at the people, "Close all the doors, there is an animal outside." The wolf starts to pound up against the door. Staff shut all the doors from the platforms. They tell everyone to get out. They then run out towards the main doors and pull down the shutters. The wolf starts to really pound against the shutters. The shutters are no match for the wolf as he breaks through and starts attacking and biting the people. The wolf goes in the direction of the town centre, the place where the wolf disappears.

The police and the armed cops arrive on the scene. However, the wolf has run off in the direction of the Irish Sea. Nobody knows where the wolf is in the city centre. People are told to stay indoors. However, the police know, there are plenty of people on the trams.

At this stage, the wolf starts running towards the direction of Blackpool Circus and goes running up the stairs into the circus. He starts to bite people in the audience. The audience starts to run very quickly towards the exit. The wolf starts to snap at everything in sight.

The wolf starts to run around the centre circle, looking for a way out. He starts running up the stairs. People are running out the doors, screaming very loudly.

He starts to run in the direction of the trams and manages to burst onto the carriages. He starts to attack all the passengers. The passengers start to run to the back of the train. The train stops and the doors open up. The wolf starts to run in the direction to the theatre on the pier. He runs into the theatre and starts snapping at the people. The audience starts to run out the exits of the theatre. The police surround the theatre for the wolf to come out.

The wolf comes tearing out and jumps onto the police. Lots of shots ring out and hit him a number of times. He collapses onto the deck of the pier, and he starts to transform back into a human being. The werewolf is Joe Dante.

Catherine and Richard see, from a distance, that it is Joe Dante.

Richard:

"One down, a few more werewolves and vampires to go; I think we should go back to Paula Anne to see if she has anymore gadgets so we can track down more werewolves and vampires."

Funeral Home
Dr John Landis:

"Well, fellow werewolves and vampires, I have some very sad news for you. Our friend Joe Dante was shot tonight; he is no longer with us. They did not take any chances; they used ordinary bullets to kill our friend. They dipped some of the bullets into silver to see if the bullets would work. This is the closest they could come to get a silver bullet. It worked; the silver that was dipped did the trick.

However, we will continue with our plan. We will take over the armies of the world. This is only a blip in our plan for world domination of certain armies."

Vampires:

All the vampires start to cry out, "No, no, no. Even if we are vampires, we loved Joe as if he was one of us."

Una:

"I really want to go after Richard and Catherine. I think they can do us a lot of damage."

Rochelle:

"I think Vanessa has a soft spot for Richard. I think she wants him all for herself."

Vanessa:

"I do, there is something about him. I would not like anything to happen to him."

Frankie:

"What about Catherine, she can do us a lot of harm?"

Mollie:

"I agree with Nadine, let's kill both of them. However, we will get our own back on the residents and the police for shooting Joe. Tomorrow night, we will attack the audience at the ice-skating show."

Una:

"I agree, that sounds like a good idea. We will not be messed about with. Let's take our revenge tomorrow night."

Ice Rink Show

The seats are filled with about twenty percent of people. The venue is really cold.

Richard:

"I have a funny feeling that the vampires will come here tonight. They will probably start looking for some kind of revenge."

Catherine:

"I hate your funny feelings, something nasty happens when you get them."

Just behind them, the two of them hear a hissing sound. "Hello, Catherine and Richard, have you come to enjoy the show?"

Catherine:

"I don't believe it Richard, Faye, Claire, and Lisa are behind us."

Faye:

"Enjoy the show; it looks like your last."

Claire:

"You will never defeat us. It doesn't matter if you have all the police and soldiers behind you. We have too much intelligence for you to outwit us."

Lisa:

"The biggest mistake was when you killed the werewolf. We may be vampires; killing one of them is like murdering one of us."

Richard:

"Where are your girlfriends with the fangs?"

Faye:

"You'll soon find out. In fact, the audience is in for a big surprise tonight."

The show starts and all the ice skaters come out in their costumes. They are all covered in costumes. It is very difficult to figure out who the dancers are.

Richard:

"Look Catherine, all the vampires are in the line-up."

At this moment, the vampires look up at Richard and Catherine, showing their teeth. They then start to skate around and start to do the dance.

Then the vampires start to bite their fellow dancers. Members of the audience start to scream. The vampires start to pounce on the audience. The audience start to run in all directions, screaming and trampling over people.

Vanessa:

"The ordinary people are simply no match for us. I want to enjoy tonight sucking the throats of all the people tonight, or as many as I can get my teeth into."

Nadine:

"I will take care of Catherine. I do not have any time for competition from fellow females. I want to have her for supper. I am quite hungry and thirsty."

Faye:

"Right, we will attack Catherine in a couple of nights. We will then decide what to do with Richard. Vanessa seems to want him for herself."

Anna:

"I say let's kill Richard and Catherine. I have had enough of the two of them."

Nadine:

"We will let Richard and Catherine go for the moment. We have plenty of people to choose from tonight."

At this moment, the vampires start to attack more of the audience. They start to pick them up and start flying with them into the air.

People start running out of the arena into the amusement area.

Richard:

"Let's go towards the exit, Catherine."

Richard and Catherine go running towards the rollercoaster. They see one is about to leave the starting point. The two of them jump into the seat. The rollercoaster is at the starting area. Richard and Catherine jump into the seats. The ride starts off going up and then going down the rollercoaster. They are going up and down and from side to side. They don't know that Faye and Nadine are behind them in the next car.

Catherine:

"If the ride does not kill us, the two behind us will."

Richard:

"This will buy us time to get our thinking caps on. The vampires are running everywhere."

The ride comes to a standstill and the two of them go running in the direction of the trams.

Catherine:

"Let's jump onto the tram and see what happens."

At this stage, Richard and Catherine jump onto the tram. The doors shut and they see the vampires flying past the windows, looking in through the windows.

The doors open, and all of the vampires come inside and start attacking the passengers. Blood splatter is going all over the carriage.

Richard:

"As soon as the next station comes, we will get off."

Richard:

"Why are you looking at Catherine in that way, Vanessa?"

Vanessa:

"I am trying to figure out when I am going to have Catherine all to myself. I do not know if I want to kill the two of you. You are so much fun to have around. You are like members of our family. You can always come to our side and have a bite to eat every night. You could say it is a healthy diet.

The door is about to open I want the two of you to go back to your hotel. I do not want to kill you both now. I am beginning to become quite fond of the two of you."

Catherine:

"Quickly, let's go before she changes her mind."

Back at the hotel:

Richard:

"I wonder why she let us go. I think deep down, they do not want to harm us."

Funeral Home
Dr John Landis:

"Well, ladies, I know you had a good time tonight getting your feed. Why did you not kill Richard and Catherine?"

Lisa:

"We had a little chat amongst us girls and we are getting very fond of Richard and Catherine. Deep down, we want them to come to our side. Richard can get us all pregnant. Catherine can also have vampire children and there will be more of us to take over the world."

Dr John Landis:

"That sounds like a good idea. However, our time in Blackpool is about to come to an end. I want to go to the Isle of Wight and the Isle of Mull to hide out and carry out our plan.

First, we will go to the Isle of Wight. There will be plenty of victims there for us."

Rochelle:

"What about the werewolves, we need more of them?"

Dr John Landis:

"Don't worry, with my potion, I can inject more victims or when I turn into a werewolf, I will attack more people."

Claire:

"That sounds like a good idea. Let's get some rest for our travels to the islands."

Rochelle:

"First, we will have to take care of Paula Anne, the private investigator, she knows too much about us."

Private Investigator Office

Mollie starts to hover outside, waiting for Paula Anne to arrive. Paula arrives at the office, and Mollie looks at her.

Mollie:

"I have been waiting for you for a long time. I thought you would never come. You have caused us nothing but trouble."

Mollie reaches and with her hand she hits Paula Anne sideways. Paula Anne goes flying into the air and hits a car. At this stage, the rest of the vampires attack Paula Anne for their feed.

Faye:

"Right, tomorrow we will go to the Isle of Wight. We will blend in there." We can find more victims. The next night, they start to fly down by the Irish Sea, down towards southern England. They know that the doctor will transport their coffins for them to sleep in.

Army Headquarters
Tom Holland:

"I am the new head of command. We know that we have a werewolf and vampire problem in this country. They have caused mayhem in Blackpool. The British Army cannot go on the national media and tell them that we have a problem we can't get deal with.

With our intelligence, we know that Dr John Landis will try to turn more people into werewolves with the help of his lady vampires. We have bugged wherever they stay and they are off to the Isle of Wight.

I have a funny feeling that they want to turn the Isle of Wight into a residence for female vampires and werewolves. We have to stop them carrying out this deed.

Dr John Landis:

"Well, ladies, I have decided we can hide out in this abandoned holiday camp called Harcourt Sands. Very few people come here so we can plan our attack of the people here. They will not know what will happen to them when we attack them. If everyone who lives can be turned into werewolves and vampires. This island can be ours to do what we wish."

Army Headquarters
Tom Holland:

"As you know, I am in charge. I have been informed by the Irish Army and the officers and soldiers in the British Army that we have a werewolves and vampires. We do not want to alert the general public of this. We know, from our sources, that the werewolves and the vampires are residing on the Isle of Wight.

There is a good chance that if they start to attack the residents of the island, they too will become infected and the Isle of Wight will be run by werewolves and vampires. If this happens, we will have to cut the people off from the mainland.

We will be sending soldiers to the isle as soon as the vampires start to attack the people. With the werewolves, they will be able to take over the island in a short period of time."

Isle of Wight
Faye:

"Right, girls, I have had enough of taking it easy. I am thirsty and hungry. It has been a while since I have had something to fill my hunger. I want more vampires amongst us. This is nothing personal girls, but after a while it gets a bit boring, talking to the same vampires on a nightly basis."

Mollie:

"I totally agree with you, but we are going to have to go after Richard and Catherine. They have lived far too long. All of us should have drunk some of Richard's and Catherine's blood.

Let's get started when they arrive. I am sure it will not be too long before they land on the island."

Isle of Wight
Richard:

"It is great to be here, I thought we would never get here. We have to book into a hotel tonight. We will then have to get our act together and get rid of the vampires."

Catherine:

"I will get the stakes, garlic and holy cross ready for tomorrow night. I will have to get some silver for the werewolves. I do not think they will have any silver bullets here. So it is the next best thing for getting rid of them."

Tom Holland:

"Well, lads, tomorrow night we are going to attack the Isle of Wight; there will be a full moon tomorrow night. The night will also be time for the vampires. Now we are going to mine the most important bridges near the harbours."

The Next Night

The werewolves start to change and start attacking people all over the island. The vampires start to do the same. People are running all over the place. The residents start jumping into their motor vehicles. They aren't able to escape; they are attacked from all sides by the werewolves and vampires.

Richard and Catherine start to run along the roads. All the residents in the local area start running all over the place. Some get attacked by the vampires; they are no match for them. Richard and Catherine run into the local bus station.

Richard:

"Is there anyone around who can drive a bus quickly? There are vampires outside and we will need a bus for safety."

Bus Driver:

"Come over here, we can use this bus. I will get this bus out of the garage as soon as possible."

The driver starts up the ignition and starts to drive out of the garage with Richard and Catherine.

The bus starts to go along the roads of the local area. The vampires start to see the bus and sense Richard and Catherine are both on the bus.

Mollie:

"Quickly, they are trying to escape. Let's finish the two of them off now. I am fed up with them. They have caused nothing but trouble since we met them."

Una:

"I would love to finish them off now."

The bus is tearing down the side roads, trying to get to the local ferry. The Isle of Wight is in a state of chaos. The British Army is on the island, trying to restore law and order. The bus starts swerving all over the road, trying to avoid the werewolves and vampires.

The bus starts driving in the direction of the ferry. Richard and Catherine can see behind them that a lot of the island is in flames. The British Army is doing their best to bring the island under their control.

Richard:

"We have to get onto the ferry, or else we have had it."

Catherine:

"Instead of us getting onto the ferry, we should see if we can get some person on a boat to go to the Isle of Mull off the coast of Scotland. They will not think twice about following us there."

They get to the port and the soldiers get out of the bus and run towards the boat.

Richard:

"Hello, to everyone on the boat. As you can see, the island is under attack. We have to go to the Isle of Mull, can you take us there?"

Ian Watkins:

"Come on over, we better get going, those werewolves and vampires will not be long getting here. The Isle of Wight has fallen to the werewolves and the vampires."

Lee Latchford:

"That's right! We are going to the Isle of Mull. Hop on board everyone, including the soldiers. The weather may turn rough in an hour or so.

It will take us a few hours to get to the Isle of Mull. Hopefully the werewolves will not get us."

Isle of Wight:

The vampires and the werewolves arrive at the ferry port. They start to see the boat going out towards the sea.

Dr John Landis:

"I wonder where they are going at this time of night. I do not think it is the mainland."

Vanessa:

"I am worn out flying, I need a break. We are going to have to take over a boat and follow them. We will need a captain to go after them. Let's see, there is a large boat over there, we could take charge of."

The vampires and the some of the werewolves get onto the boat.

Vanessa:

"Hello captain and what is your name?"

Captain:

"My name is Ike, and I am the captain of this boat."

Vanessa:

"Well, if you want to live, I suggest you go after that boat."

Ike:

"Very well then, I will go after them now."

Mollie:

"I feel as if the weather is going to change. We better take cover in this boat."

At this stage, the sea changes, and it gets very rough. A lot of rain comes down on them.

Rochelle:

"Wherever they are going, we will have to find a place to lay low for a while."

Frankie:

"I think that is a good idea. We will have to figure out how to turn more people into vampires and werewolves. The Isle of Wight has fallen to us."

Mollie:

"We have been going for hours. Let's check the map and see if the captain can figure out where we are going."

Ike:

"I have a funny feeling that they are going to the Isle of Mull. They can dock their small boat there."

Mollie:

"I think you could be right. There will only be a small number of people on the island."

Isle of Mull

It is very stormy as they try to dock their boat. The seas are rough.

Richard:

"We better find a place where we can stay. The vampires and werewolves will not take long in tracking us down. I think this is the place where we can finish them off."

Catherine:

"We will have to check into a local hotel. This is the best we can do for the moment. We will tell the locals that the werewolves and vampires that they saw on the news, taking over the Isle of Wight, are here to take over the Isle of Mull.

Hotel

Richard and Catherine check into the hotel.

Receptionist:

"How can I help you?"

Richard:

"Let's start by getting all the locals into the hotel bar."

Receptionist:

"Why all the fuss?"

Catherine:

"It is to warn the people of the vampires and werewolves coming to the Isle of Mull."

Receptionist:

"Right, I will text all the hotel guests and surrounding business to let them know."

Later on, that night
Richard:

"Good evening ladies and gentlemen. As you can see from what happened in the Isle of Wight, we have a serious problem on our hands. The werewolves and vampires are behind us. It will not be long before they are here. They want more victims so they can take over the world."

"We will have to be careful. We may be on our own for the next few days. We can't rely on the army."

Catherine:

"For those of you in the hotel, stay indoors. All outsiders should go home and lock their doors until the morning. All of us should have enough time to get inside before they get here."

Hotel

At this stage, all the people, excluding the guests, start to leave to go on their way home. Some leave with instruments, in case they get attacked.

Later on, in the hotel, the guests start to hear strange noises. A fog descends on the area, which makes everything hard to see.

Richard:

"The way I see it, ladies and gentlemen, we will have to stay in the foyer. There's only about twenty of us here. So, it would not be too hard for us to keep an eye out for one another."

They hear a howl coming from outside the windows.

Catherine:

"I guess that means only one thing; our friend Dr John Landis is near and he wants a few more members for his little club of werewolves."

Richard:

"I have a funny feeling that the sexy, naughty, bitches will be close by. It is proving to be a major problem, getting rid of those vampires."

Guests:

"What are we going to do? We can't go up against them. The army and the police will be no match for them. Richard and Catherine, do your best in defeating the werewolves and vampires. Don't cry for us, we will do our best and if the worst comes to the worst. Well, we have had a nice life and we all heard that heaven isn't all that bad."

Richard:

"Put on Nessun Dorma, play it very loud. We will all go out in a blaze of glory. Let's show them we mean business."

At this stage, the song is put on repeat, so it will let all the vampires and werewolves know we mean business.

The Interior of the Hotel

At this stage, the vampires and werewolves come crashing through the windows.

Faye:

"It's all nice of you to be here in one place. This is really mannerly of you all; considering this will be the last night you will see. Which one of us do you want? Who says that vampires are courteous? We do have a sense of humour.

Vanessa:

"Any takers on the offer of 'once bitten, twice shy'?
"No, not one, that is terrible."

Mollie:

"Well, girls we gave them their chance. Let's have a few members for our club. I'd rather have a few more members in our club than more werewolves."

At this stage, the vampires start attacking all the guests in the hotel. Nadine, Faye, Lisa and Claire start throwing some of them against the windows. They start tearing them apart.

Vanessa:

"Catherine is mine, don't touch her. I want her, she has caused so much trouble."

At this stage, Vanessa starts to tear her apart, and Catherine starts to scream in agony.

Catherine:

"You're tearing me apart, Richard, help me please."

Richard:

Richard sees that there is no way he can help Catherine. "Sorry Catherine, I can't do anything."

Catherine:

"Run Richard, get away, as fast as you can."
Richard runs out the door, into the path of Faye.

Faye:

"You didn't think it was going to be that easy, did you? I have wanted you for a very long time."

Richard:

"If it wasn't for the nights, as some people would say, I would love to be a vampire."

Faye:

"It is nice to see that you still have a sense of humour, Richard. Do you honestly believe the authorities will let you and Catherine back to live in Ireland or England?

You know too much for them now. They will probably kill you. They will do the same to Catherine. However, if you come to our side, you will live life like you have never lived before."

At this point, Faye starts to hover around Richard.

Richard:

"I don't have a choice, now do I? If I leave, I will surely be killed. Faye, do what you have to do. Bring me to your side. However, make sure what you have to do is nice and gentle. I do not like pain."

Faye:

"That is the best news that I have heard all night. I was hoping you would come to our side without any fuss. Life would suck without you."

At this point, Faye starts to go up and down Richard's neck, and sinks her fangs into his neck. Richard screams out in pain.

Richard is lying on the ground, and then he comes to his senses. His teeth start to come out and his eyes start to change colour.

Richard:

"I guess now, Faye, it is time to start the night shift."

Faye:

"Come with me and I will give you some flying lessons."

Richard:

"Let's go for Catherine and we will see if she wants to join our team."

Catherine:

"Oh my God, there is Richard, flying with Faye. He has turned."

Richard and Faye land, as well as Vanessa.

Vanessa:

"Well Catherine, do you not think it is time to join us?"

Catherine:

I don't think that I have any choice. The authorities will not let me leave this island with all the secrets.

Vanessa:

"Come to me for a quick bite, and now it is time for your throat to meet my teeth. I have bitten you earlier, now it is time for the final bite, to turn you completely into a vampire."

At this point, Catherine screams and turns into a vampire.

Richard:

"What do we do now?"

Faye:

"We will go after Dr John Landis."

Dr John Landis:

"Well it is nice to see that Richard and Catherine have decided to join the team. We will have to stay here until the time is right, to leave with the other vampires and werewolves. It will be a while, because the authorities have blocked all exits."

At this point, the rest of the vampires arrive; Lisa, Claire, Mollie, Frankie, Una, Vanessa and Rochelle.

Dr John Landis:

"Welcome ladies, now we will just have to wait and see what will happen to us."

The next morning, the following announcement is announced on the radio. The Isle of Mull and the Isle of Wight have been closed off. This is in the interest of our society. All military will patrol the island and everyone on the islands will have to stay there.

Faye:

"Only time will tell what will happen to us."

The End